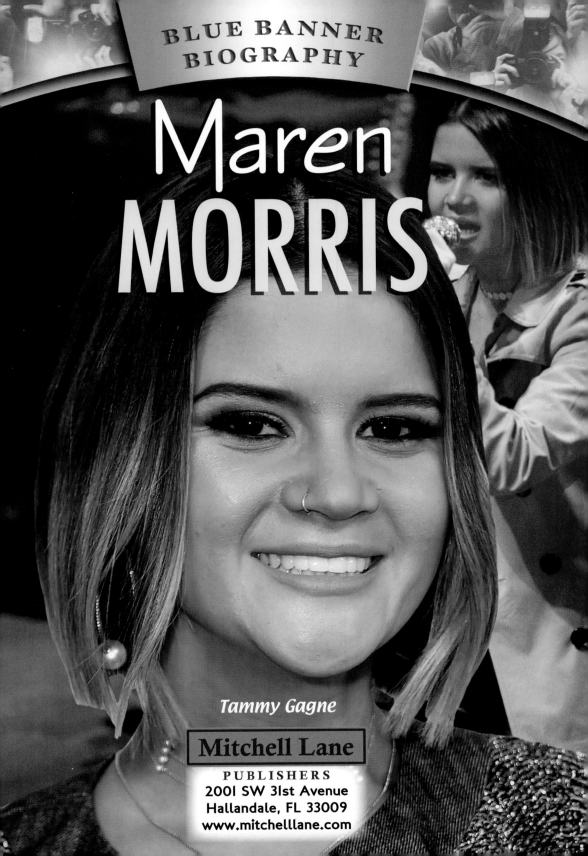

BLUE BANNER
BIOGRAPHY

Maren MORRIS

Tammy Gagne

Mitchell Lane
PUBLISHERS
2001 SW 31st Avenue
Hallandale, FL 33009
www.mitchelllane.com

Mitchell Lane
PUBLISHERS

Printing   1   2   3   4   5   6   7   8   9

Blue Banner Biographies

5 Seconds of Summer	Gwen Stefani	Mary-Kate and Ashley Olsen
Aaron Judge	Hope Solo	Megan Fox
Abby Wambach	Ice Cube	Miguel Tejada
Adele	Jamie Foxx	Mike Trout
Alicia Keys	James Harden	Nancy Pelosi
Allen Iverson	Jared Goff	Natasha Bedingfield
Ashanti	Ja Rule	Nicki Minaj
Ashlee Simpson	Jason Derulo	One Direction
Ashton Kutcher	Jay-Z	Orianthi
Avril Lavigne	Jennifer Hudson	Orlando Bloom
Blake Lively	Jennifer Lopez	P. Diddy
Blake Shelton	Jessica Simpson	Peyton Manning
Bow Wow	JJ Watt	Pharrell Williams
Brett Favre	J. K. Rowling	Pit Bull
Britney Spears	John Legend	Prince William
CC Sabathia	Justin Berfield	Queen Latifah
Carrie Underwood	Justin Timberlake	Robert Downey Jr.
Carson Wentz	Kanye West	Ron Howard
Charlie Puth	Kate Hudson	Russell Westbrook
Chris Brown	Keith Urban	Russell Wilson
Chris Daughtry	Kelly Clarkson	Sean Kingston
Christina Aguilera	Kenny Chesney	Selena
Clay Aiken	Ke$ha	Shia LaBeouf
Cole Hamels	Kevin Durant	Shontelle Layne
Condoleezza Rice	Kristen Stewart	Soulja Boy Tell 'Em
Corbin Bleu	Lady Gaga	Stephenie Meyer
Daniel Radcliffe	Lance Armstrong	Taylor Swift
David Ortiz	Leona Lewis	T.I.
David Wright	Le'Veon Bell	Timbaland
Derek Hough	Lindsay Lohan	Tim McGraw
Derek Jeter	LL Cool J	Toby Keith
Drew Brees	Ludacris	Usher
Dwyane Wade	Luke Bryan	Vanessa Anne Hudgens
Eminem	Maren Morris	The Weeknd
Eve	Mariah Carey	Will.i.am
Fergie	Mario	Zac Efron
Flo Rida	Mary J. Blige	

Library of Congress Cataloging-in-Publication Data
Names: Gagne, Tammy, author.
Title: Maren Morris / by Tammy Gagne.
Description: Hallandale, FL : Mitchell Lane Publishers, [2018] | Series: Blue banner biographies | Includes bibliographical references and index.
Identifiers: LCCN 2017050212 | ISBN 9781680201826 (library bound) | ISBN 9781680201833 (ebook)
Subjects: LCSH: Morris, Maren--Juvenile literature. | Country musicians--United States--Biography--Juvenile literature.
Classification: LCC ML3930.M8 G34 2018 | DDC 782.421642092 [B] --dc23
LC record available at https://lccn.loc.gov/2017050212

ABOUT THE AUTHOR: Tammy Gagne has written more than 200 books for both adults and children. Her recent titles include several books about country music artists—including Dierks Bentley and Kacey Musgraves. She resides in northern New England with her husband and son.

PUBLISHER'S NOTE: The following story has been thoroughly researched and to the best of our knowledge represents a true story. While every possible effort has been made to ensure accuracy, the publisher will not assume liability for damages caused by inaccuracies in the data and makes no warranty on the accuracy of the information contained herein. This story has not been authorized or endorsed by Maren Morris.

Blue Banner Biography

There's a reason Maren Morris looks so comfortable on stage. She has been performing in front of audiences since her early teenage years. Now she plays at benefits like this one at the Country Music Hall of Fame and Museum.

"**M**om! Can I borrow your guitar?" asked Andrea's daughter Jaime.

Andrea hadn't thought about the instrument in years. But as she made her way to the hallway closet where she kept it, a smile started spreading across her face. Oh, how she had loved playing that acoustic guitar! She often used it to sing Jaime to sleep when she was a toddler. Now Jaime was in the eighth grade. That old guitar hadn't seen the light of day since she was in elementary school.

"Sure," Andrea said as she shoved the coats and jackets aside so Jaime could reach the tall black case. "Do you want to learn how to play it?"

"Nope. I just need it as a prop," Jaime answered as she spotted her mom's white leather jacket. It had called the closet home even longer than the guitar. "Ooh, and how about this? Could I borrow this, too? Tomorrow is Eighties Day at school, and I want to go as Maren Morris."

Andrea had to chuckle. "You do realize that Maren Morris wasn't even alive during the eighties, right?"

"Of course she wasn't!" Jaime answered, rolling her eyes for a moment before catching herself. She knew

that her mom hated it when she rolled her eyes. "But Maren Morris sings that song '80s Mercedes.' I found Dad's old Mercedes keychain in the junk drawer, and I'm going to wear it on the belt of my jeans. What do you think?"

To Andrea, playing a guitar was just like riding a bike.

"I think you should let me give you a guitar lesson. No sense in carrying around a guitar all day if you can't play a single chord. Can you let me listen to that song? Maybe I can teach you a bit of it."

To Andrea, playing a guitar was just like riding a bike. Even though it had been years since she had strummed her Fender six-string, she could still play it as easily as ever. People said she had an ear for music. She could hear a song on the radio and pick out the chords in just a few minutes. She taught herself to play when she was a teenager herself.

"How long do you think it would take me to learn the whole song?" Jaime asked anxiously.

"It could take some time," Andrea cautioned. "But if you keep working at it, you could learn that one and many more. You don't think Maren Morris learned to play overnight, do you? I've read that she was about your age when she started playing."

"I'd love to be able to play like her," Jaime said. She scrolled through the songs on her smartphone before finding "80s Mercedes" and hitting Play. After listening to the melody, Andrea started strumming the chorus and singing along to the catchy tune.

"Hey, you're pretty good at that," Jaime said, sounding a bit shocked. She had forgotten how talented her mother was. "You really think I could learn it?"

"I sure do," Andrea assured her. She knew her daughter could do anything she set her mind to accomplishing.

"Maybe we could have a lesson each night, if you want," Jaime suggested.

"I think that sounds like a great idea," Andrea replied. "Now let's see what we can do about finding my old Wayfarer sunglasses for you. They go great with that jacket."

✳ ✳ ✳ ✳

Maren Morris burst onto the country music scene in January, 2016 with her digital single, "My Church." The song compared listening to music while driving to a religious experience. Apparently, many listeners could relate to Maren's take. The song received 2.5 million streams in about a month. She recorded her first mainstream

album, *Hero*, a year later. It too was a hit, reaching the top spot on the Top Country Albums chart. Maren is part of a new movement in country music that embraces individuality. She doesn't try to sound like other successful artists. "There are so many times I turn on the radio and I hear a guy and I have no idea who it is because it sounds like four other people," she told *Rolling Stone* in 2016. Maren doesn't worry what people will think of her. She simply writes and records music from her heart. Her songs reflect her personality and talent. And her fans respond to that honesty by buying her music and showing up at her concerts. She has also earned herself an Academy of Country Music (ACM) award, a Country Music Association (CMA) award, and a Grammy.

Grammy

2

A Natural Talent

Kellie and Scott Morris welcomed their daughter Maren Larae Morris on April 10, 1990 in Dallas, Texas. The couple gave Maren a baby sister named Karsen three years later. The family owns a hair salon in nearby Arlington, which they have named Maren Karsen Aveda Salon for their daughters. The girls basically grew up at the business, playing in the back room when they were younger and working at the front desk as they got older.

As with many hair salons, music is always playing in the background. As a child, Maren would sing along to the songs. But no one realized what a powerful voice she had until one day when she was nine. The salon often hosted barbecues and holiday parties. Maren's godfather brought a karaoke machine to one of these parties. When Maren tried it out, her family members were stunned by her singing talent. "We were like, 'Wow, that's coming out of her,'" her dad told Jeff Gage of the *Dallas Observer*. "It kind of floored us. We were like, 'Hmm, there's something there. We might want to pursue that.'"

"Pursue that" her parents did. They bought her a guitar and encouraged her to write songs as she learned

Maren and mom Kellie at the 59th Grammy Awards. Maren won the Best Country Solo Performance for "My Church."

how to play it. They also bought their own karaoke machine—something not many people had at that time. By the time she was 14, she had mastered the guitar and wanted to start performing in front of real audiences.

While Maren was learning guitar chords, Kellie and Scott began learning about the music business. They helped their daughter get started by taking her to local honky-tonks and other venues where she could play for the crowds. One of those venues was The Grease Monkey Burger Shop & Social Club in Arlington. She played there every Thursday for two years for $100 a night.

Maren's parents also helped her self-release her first album, *Walk On*, in 2005. She quickly attracted the attention of music distributors. Maren recorded her second album, *All That It Takes*, two years later. She worked with Smith Music Group on the project to ensure that people could download its songs at all the popular music sites. In addition to singing and playing the guitar, Maren was also becoming a skilled songwriter. She wrote or co-wrote eight of the 13 songs on *All That It Takes*.

Maren's parents also helped her enter talent shows—including the popular television shows *American Idol,*

> **Maren's parents also helped her self-release her first album, Walk On, in 2005.**

Nashville Star, and *The Voice*. She didn't have much luck, though. The shows all rejected her. At the time she was heartbroken. No one realized at that time that contestants of both *American Idol* and *The Voice* would sing covers of Maren's song "My Church" just a few years later. Her ultimate rise to stardom shows that determination pays off. And she has never been in short supply of that quality.

As a young girl, Maren's biggest idol was fellow Texan LeAnn Rimes, who had become a successful country music star in her early teens. Maren said that watching someone just a few years older than she was strike it big made her dream of becoming a country singer feel like it was within her reach. Her other early influences included Sheryl Crow, the Spice Girls, and the boy band N*SYNC.

In addition to music, Maren showed great talent for creative writing, drawing, and acting. Unlike many young people, she always felt comfortable on stage. Whenever she appeared in a theater

LeAnn Rimes

production, she knew that people would be judging her performance. She learned to put up a wall that protected her from any negativity. That wall freed her to give her very best without worrying about how others reacted.

When she was 15, Maren received an opportunity to attend a Grammy camp in Los Angeles. It allowed her to meet and take workshops with some of the biggest names in the music business—including David Foster, Paul Williams, and Jimmy Jam. She had never flown in an airplane when she traveled to the West Coast for the camp.

Maren graduated from James Bowie High School in Arlington before moving on to the University of North Texas. But she only stayed there one semester. She knew she wanted to pursue a career in music. She was doing a lot of traveling around Texas to give performances. But she was tired of that and wanted to try something else. Her friend Kacey Musgraves, who was also chasing the dream of becoming a country music star, encouraged Maren to relocate to Nashville. Musgraves told her that the Tennessee city offered great potential for people interested in writing songs for established country artists. In 2013, Maren packed everything she owned into a U-Haul and made the move.

Kacey Musgraves

3 Finding Her Voice

Maren gave herself a deadline of one year to find a job as a country songwriter in Nashville. If she hadn't been hired by a songwriting house by then, she would return home. Well before that year was up, however, Maren met Carla Wallace of Big Yellow Dog Music. Wallace offered her a contract.

Maren quickly learned that the songwriting process in Nashville was a team effort. She began collaborating with other songwriters. By this time, she felt burned out from all the performing she had been doing in Texas. She loved the idea of putting her talent and creativity to work for other artists instead of having to get up on stage herself. In no time at all, she had written songs for big-name artists such as Tim McGraw and Kelly Clarkson.

Wallace became increasingly impressed with the material that Maren turned out. But there was something that stopped her from wanting to pitch it to other country artists. Her songs had a unique quality. Not just anyone could do them justice. Soon, Wallace realized that the best person to sing Maren's songs was Maren herself. They fit her personality and voice perfectly.

Maren was starting to feel the same way. She related especially strongly to "My Church." When she and Wallace took a road trip together in California, they listened to a demo Maren had recorded of the song. They didn't want anyone else to record it. When Maren returned to Nashville, she decided to record the song, along with four others which she self-released.

As soon as she released the extended play version of "My Church," people everywhere began streaming it. In addition to expanding her fan base, all this play time nabbed the attention of many people in the recording business. Several labels wanted to sign her. But she knew

Maren's song "My Church" went platinum. This means that it sold more than one million copies.

she didn't need to take the first offers she received. She decided to wait until just the right one arrived. That offer came in 2016 from Columbia Nashville. The company wanted Maren to record a full-length album right away—and to do it her own way. The result was *Hero*.

Critics praised Maren as a fresh new voice in country music. Each song she released was unlike all the others, yet in keeping with her style. Even people who didn't listen to country music listened to Maren Morris. She was doing something few country singers ever manage—crossing over into pop music. *Rolling Stone* even named *Hero* as one of the Best 50 Albums of 2016.

When Maren won the CMA Best New Artist of the Year Award, fans gathered at The Grease Monkey to celebrate their hometown heroine. The people in Arlington were not the least bit surprised that Maren had made it in the world of country music. Everyone there who had heard her sing knew

Maren holding her 2016 CMA Award for Best New Artist of the Year in November, 2016

Also in 2016, Keith Urban invited Maren to open for him on his RipCORD World Tour.

that she was something special. Now others had discovered that as well.

Also in 2016, Keith Urban invited Maren to open for him on his RipCORD World Tour. She knew she had accomplished something huge when the tour took her to her home state. During her performance at the American Airlines Center in Dallas, Maren removed her earpiece to sing an a cappella part of "My Church." Removing the device allowed her to hear all her fans sing the words along with her. The song that meant so much to her had also hit home with her audience.

Maren performing on Keith Urban's RipCORD World Tour

Maren performs with Keith Urban and Brett Eldredge during the 2016 CMT Music Awards.

On the last night of the tour, Maren decided to pull a fun prank on Urban. He stood on the stage, waiting for her to join him for his song "We Were Us." But instead of Maren, her drummer Christian Paschall came out—dressed in her costume. When Paschall opened his mouth, the audience heard Maren's voice. She had hidden backstage and sang into the live microphone as Paschall lip-synced her part of the song. Urban laughed so hard that he fell onto the stage. Maren had already shown that she had talent. Now her fans were seeing that she had a sense of humor as well.

> **She knew she had accomplished something huge when the tour took her to her home state.**

4 Singing Her Truth

Country music fans see something in Maren Morris that is different from other artists. She thinks part of what fans find so refreshing is her fresh female viewpoint. The world of country music is filled with male singers and songwriters. Of course, the genre has its share of female stars. But Maren feels that most female country stars don't sing about subjects that matter to her. It seems to her that they focus on things like wanting a cute boy to notice them or being dumped. So she doesn't sing about the self-pity of having her heart broken. Instead, she sings about where she is in her life right now. Many people her age can relate to her music for this reason.

Maren also thinks that the newest wave of country artists has added some much-needed diversity to the genre. She feels that in addition to more women, country music needs a wider range of styles.

She is the first person to admit that her songs do not all fall within the category of country. One of the things that Maren admires most about Sheryl Crow is that she broke down the walls among the various music genres with her music. Maren was only three years old when Crow released her first album, *Tuesday Night*

> **Even big stars enjoy meeting their idols.**

Music Club. But she grew up listening to it. And she paid attention. Crow doesn't fit into a box. Her music includes sounds of pop, rock, and country. Maren saw her as creating her own genre.

Even though she is now a big star, Maren says that she is still learning and growing as an artist. Instead of putting up the wall that used to protect her from negativity, she has started opening up more in front of her audiences. When she first began performing, she focused on her singing. Now she understands that part of her job is engaging the crowd. She has more fun when she is on stage now. Doing so has allowed her to feel uplifted by the crowds. And that feeling makes her performances even better.

Even big stars enjoy meeting their idols. Maren admits that she has always had a huge crush on Bruce Springsteen. But until recently she had never gotten the chance to see him perform live. It turns out that her

Bruce Springsteen

Maren performs on Season 42 of **Saturday Night Live** *in December, 2016.*

music director, Max Weinberg, is also Springsteen's drum tech. Weinberg arranged for Maren to see The Boss in concert. Following the show, Maren told David Browne of *Rolling Stone* how much his performance inspired her. "After seeing him play four hours," she said, "I was like, 'I have no excuse to perform an off show.'"

Maren's rise up the music charts also gave her the opportunity to perform as a musical guest on *Saturday Night Live*. After singing "My Church" and "80s Mercedes" during the live music portion of the comedy show, Maren got to meet the show's creator, Lorne Michaels. As an *SNL* fan, meeting Michaels had long been on her bucket list. The famous producer told her that his daughter also lives in Nashville.

One of Maren's most surprising encounters with one of her idols, though, came in the form of a phone call. When Maren checked her phone one day, she noticed that she had two missed calls from a number she did not recognize. The caller's location was South London. Her manager later informed her that Elton John had been trying to get in touch with her. Luckily, he called again. This time, Maren answered. John wanted to tell her how much he enjoyed her music. He even said that he owned a copy of *Hero* on vinyl.

In 2018, Maren got to honor one of her idols in a special way. She performed as part of the "Elton John: I'm Still Standing—A Grammy Salute" two days after the Grammy Award show.

5 An Incredible Ride

Maren has teamed up with many songwriting partners over the years. One is Ryan Hurd. Although the two worked for different publishing houses, their bosses put them together one day to see what would happen. The result was a ballad called "Last Turn Home." It is one of the first songs that Maren sold after arriving in Nashville. When country megastar Tim McGraw heard the song, he liked it so much that he decided to record it the very next day. That songwriting session with Hurd helped change Maren's life in more ways than one.

The two songwriters continued working together. In addition to clicking as writers, they also became good friends. Maren said that she found it helpful to be with someone who could relate to her frequently crazy life. Over the next two years, they realized that there was more between them than friendship. They also had romantic chemistry. They decided to date.

Finding the time for romance wasn't easy for two people with such busy careers. Like Maren, Hurd also began recording his own music since those early days in Nashville. Their relationship inspired his song "Love in a Bar."

Maren won the Publisher's Pick award at the 2017 Association of Independent Music Publishers (AIMP) Nashville Awards.

In July of 2017, Hurd asked Maren to marry him. The couple was celebrating Independence Day at his family's lake house in Michigan. Although Hurd had been carrying the engagement ring around with him for a while, he had trouble getting Maren alone. Finally, he took her for a boat ride on the lake. He proposed amidst the fireworks.

Some famous couples make flashy announcements when they

Like Maren, Hurd also began recording his own music since those early days in Nashville.

The month after they got engaged in 2017, Maren and Ryan Hurd attended the ACM Awards together in Nashville.

get engaged. But Maren and her new fiancé simply posted a photo of her ringed finger on Instagram with the word "Yes." She later confided during a CMT interview that she had no idea the proposal was coming. She was wearing sweats and her glasses at the time, implying that she would have dressed up had she suspected anything.

In her spare time, Maren enjoys lending her name and voice to help people in need. In April, 2017, she performed at the second annual Country Cares for Kids Concert. Country Cares is an organization that benefits charities such as the St. Jude Children's Research Hospital. Patients who receive treatment from this hospital never have to pay for medical services, travel, housing, or even food.

Maren enjoys lending her voice to good causes, like this concert for St. Jude Children's Research Hospital.

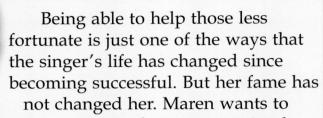

Being able to help those less fortunate is just one of the ways that the singer's life has changed since becoming successful. But her fame has not changed her. Maren wants to inspire other young artists by sharing her experiences with them. In January, 2017, she wrote a lengthy post to her many Instagram followers about her first days in Nashville. It included a photo of a young Maren shortly after her arrival.

Speaking about how blessed she feels, she offered advice to her fans who are pursuing musical careers themselves. She told them how hard she worked, showing up at every meeting she was lucky enough to get. She also emphasized the importance of being oneself. "Believe in yourself and don't be afraid to be weird or different," she wrote. "Most of all, be kind. Magical things happen to those who wait for their turn patiently in the wings."

Maren has recently returned to songwriting in preparation for her next album. She wants it to be different from *Hero*. Many artists

Maren is seen here celebrating her first number-one song, "I Could Use A Love Song" with fellow songwriters Busbee, Laura Veltz, and Jimmy Robbins.

who find success with their first album try to write similar songs for their second. They hope to hold onto their success by recreating what fans liked about them in the first place. But Maren doesn't want to repeat herself. She wants to hold onto her special style while growing as an artist and offering her fans something new at the same time.

Maren wants to inspire other young artists by sharing her experiences with them.

1990   Maren Larae Morris is born on April 10.

1999   Her family discovers her musical talent.

2004   She starts performing in front of live audiences.

2005   Maren self-releases her first album, *Walk On*.

2007   She self-releases her second album, *All That It Takes*.

2008   She graduates from James Bowie High School.

2013   Maren moves to Nashville to pursue a career in country music.

2016   Maren releases "My Church," her first big hit; wins the CMA award for Best New Artist of the Year; opens for Keith Urban on his tour; releases her first studio album, *Hero*, which *Rolling Stone* names as one of the 50 Best Albums of the Year; performs as the musical guest on *Saturday Night Live*.

2017   Maren wins ACM award for New Female Vocalist of the Year and the Grammy for Best Country Solo Performance; she gets engaged to fellow country artist Ryan Hurd.

2018   Maren marries Ryan Hurd.

DISCOGRAPHY

2004   *Walk On*
2007   *All That It Takes*
2016   *Hero*

FIND OUT MORE

On the Internet

Country Music Television, Maren Morris
  http://www.cmt.com/artists/maren-morris
Maren Morris Website
  http://marenmorris.com/
St. Jude's Children's Research Hospital
  https://www.stjude.org/

WORKS CONSULTED

———. "Country Cares for St. Jude Kids." St. Jude's Radio.
http://www.stjuderadio.org/country-cares-program
———. "Is Maren Morris Nashville's Next Breakout Pop Star?"
Downtown Arlington, February 3, 2016. https://
downtownarlington.org/news/billboard-magazine-sings-
praises-maren-morris-namesake-downtown-arlington-salon/
———. "Maren Morris." *Billboard.* http://www.billboard.com/
artist/6763296/maren-morris/biography
Bistro, Josie. "Maren Morris reflects on how life has changed
since moving to Nashville." Country Common. http://
www.countrycommon.com/maren-morris-reflects-on-how-
life-has-changed-since-moving-to-nashville/
Brickey, Kelly. "Maren Morris Gives Her Honest Opinion on
Females in Country Music." Sounds Like Nashville, April 26,
2017. http://www.soundslikenashville.com/news/maren-
morris-gives-honest-opinion-females-country-music/

Browne, David. "Maren Morris Talks Grammys, Bruce Springsteen Crush, Bro-Country Fatigue." *Rolling Stone*, January 31, 2017. http://www.rollingstone.com/music/features/maren-morris-talks-grammys-bruce-springsteen-crush-w464020

Freeman, Jon. "Maren Morris on 'Voice' Rejection, Hungover Inspiration and Unruly 'Hero.'" *Rolling Stone*, June 16, 2016. http://www.rollingstone.com/music/news/maren-morris-on-voice-rejection-hungover-inspiration-and-unruly-hero-20160616

Gage, Jeff. "'This Is Not Just Country': Maren Morris On Her Jump From DFW Bar Singer to Headlining Star." *Daily Observer*, April 11, 2017. http://www.dallasobserver.com/music/the-true-story-of-country-music-star-maren-morris-rise-from-dfw-bars-to-nashville-royalty-9348705

Levy, Joe. "Meet Maren Morris: How A Nineties Pop Fan Became Country's Breakout Star." *Rolling Stone*, June 2, 2016. http://www.rollingstone.com/music/features/meet-maren-morris-how-a-nineties-pop-fan-became-countrys-breakout-star-20160601

Lewis, Randy. "Stagecoach 2017: Maren Morris looking ahead to her next album: 'I don't want to make "Hero 2."'" *Los Angeles Times*, April 30, 2017. http://www.latimes.com/entertainment/music/la-et-ms-stagecoach-maren-morris-hero-backstage-20170430-story.html

Nelson, Jeff. "Maren Morris and Boyfriend Ryan Hurd Met While Penning a Song for Tim McGraw: 'There Was Always This Writing Chemistry.'" *People*, January 19, 2017. http://people.com/country/maren-morris-met-boyfriend-ryan-hurd-writing-tim-mcgraw-song/

Petit, Stephanie. "Maren Morris Is Engaged to Ryan Hurd—See Her Ring!" *People*, July 9, 2017. http://people.com/country/maren-morris-ryan-hurd-engaged/

Reece, Kevin. "'Nothing but pride' for Maren Morris in hometown of Arlington." WFAA, November 2, 2016. http://www.wfaa.com/news/nothing-but-pride-for-maren-morris-in-hometown-of-arlington/346520892

Reuter, Annie. "Maren Morris Recalls Being Rejected by 'American Idol,' 'The Voice.'" Taste of Country, July 5, 2016. http://tasteofcountry.com/maren-morris-reality-show-rejection/

Reuter, Annie. "Ryan Hurd Shares How Maren Morris Inspired 'Love in a Bar.'" Taste of Country, July 9, 2017. http://people.com/country/maren-morris-ryan-hurd-engaged/

Stecker, Liv. "Turns Out Elton John Is a Big Maren Morris Fan." The Boot, July 5, 2017. http://theboot.com/elton-john-fan-of-maren-morris/

Stefano, Angela. "Maren Morris Had No Idea Ryan Hurd's Proposal Was Coming." The Boot, August 1, 2017. http://theboot.com/maren-morris-ryan-hurd-proposal/

Stefano, Angela. "Maren Morris Says Farewell to Tour Boss Keith Urban With a Prank." The Boot, November 22, 2016. http://theboot.com/maren-morris-pranks-keith-urban/

Vinson, Christina. "Maren Morris Tops the Charts With Country Album, 'Hero.'" The Boot, June 16, 2016. http://theboot.com/maren-morris-hero-tops-charts/

Weingarten, Christopher R. et al. "50 Best Albums of 2016." *Rolling Stone*, November 28, 2016. http://www.rollingstone.com/music/lists/50-best-albums-of-2016-w451265/maren-morris-hero-w451300

INDEX